To _____

Enjoy the cat and
mouse game between
Ashley + Randy

Temptation Kim Saul

Temptation

KEN SAIK

Library of Congress Control Number:		2011912963
ISBN:	Hardcover	978-1-4653-4058-0
	Softcover	978-1-4653-4057-3
	Ebook	978-1-4653-4059-7

This book was printed in the United States of America.

To order additional copies of this book, contact:
Xlibris Corporation
1-888-795-4274
www.Xlibris.com
Orders@Xlibris.com
92324

A Candy to Catch

The concrete sugary savoring
stimulated by a sight, a taste, a promise
may steal a child's safety

drawing them in like a magnet--
"Don't, take candy from a stranger."

Still, the adult child savors
the sweetness of a smile
generous compliments, a favor or two

sometimes softening safety senses too--
"Don't, take candy from a stranger."

Safer sweetness to savor
stretches over time with someone.
A trust relationship is the concrete sugar,
the candy to catch.

by Adam Aski

Can a simple poem such as this created by Ashley's
boyfriend tie her securely to him when a young
attractive soccer loving fan and promoter attempts to
win her favor by enriching her cruising holiday?

"It's time to get going," announced Ashley. She sat up and slipped on her sandals.

Randy watched Ashley carefully place her paperback in the bottom of her Holland America bag and put on her sunglasses. She'd spent most of the day rolling around on the lounger, working on her tan. She'd read for a while and then slept.

The sun was just starting to sink. "It's a little early to leave, isn't it?" he asked lazily. Randy could easily remain on the lounger and read for at least another half hour.

A light blue beach cover draped her pale blue-and-green bikini. "I've got a lot to do if I'm to be ready for the captain's invitational dinner tonight." There was no hesitation in her voice. She was a picture of confidence.

Randy couldn't help admiring her. *She's so decisive, so responsible.*

Sensing that Randy was torn between staying on deck and reading or accompanying her to her cabin, Ashley said, "Feel free to stay here and read. It doesn't take a guy as long to get ready as it does for a girl."

Another thing he loved about her—she placed no expectations on him. Her suggestion was reasonable; but for Randy, nothing could override spending a few more minutes with Ashley, even if it was just walking her to her cabin door. He could read a little longer in his cabin if he really wanted to. He threw his shirt on and slipped on his sandals. Together they descended four flights of stairs to the fourth deck.

"You really dressing up for this dinner?" Randy asked, a little surprised at the perceived effort she seemed to be planning.

"It's at the captain's table. It's a semiformal affair. You bet I'm going to look great," Ashley responded as they began the walk down the narrow corridor to her cabin.

"So what does *looking great* involve you doing?" he asked, becoming a little concerned.

"Well, I have to shower, get my hair styled, put on my makeup and try on a new black dress that I thought I'd never—"

"Whooa!" Randy reacted. "Hair styled? You've got an appointment?"

"Of course!" she answered, surprised at Randy's reaction. "Last night, at our dinner table, I mentioned that we wouldn't be joining the rest of the group tonight because you won an invitation to the captain's table for dinner. Mrs. Wassel was so excited for us. She'd always hoped to secure an invite, but never had. And this is her fifth cruise. She said it's a real treat. Everyone dresses up for it. When she heard I hadn't even made an appointment with the stylist on board, she said that's the first thing I should do this morning. It's a good thing I did too. There were only a couple of times left."

Unexpectedly, Ashley stopped walking. Focusing just ahead, Randy realized that the housekeeping cart in front of them must have been the cause. He'd been concerned about his lack of a wardrobe for tonight. He hadn't paid much attention to the surroundings. Ashley's searching in her Holland America bag made him look at the cabin number: 4025. That was her cabin!

"Ashley, please." He turned her to face him and then bent down on one knee. He hoped his new posture would emphasize his desperation. "Don't go all out. I didn't bring any clothes for such an occasion."

Ashley glanced to her left and saw a heavyset elderly couple waddling down the corridor. "Don't be so silly," she said nervously. "Get up." After a moment, seeing Randy's slow response, she added emphatically, "Now." She glanced back down the hall. *Too late.* They'd been seen. The old fellow smiled. Looking back at Randy, she and her red face added, "They'll think you were proposing."

Randy glanced to his right and saw both people were smiling. Grinning, he rose.

"Do you have dress pants, a white shirt, and a tie?" Randy's plight had not escaped her.

"Pants and shirt, yes, but no tie. And I've no sport jacket either."

"Then go to the shop on the fifth deck. Buy that navy cardigan that you liked."

"The one with the Holland America logo?"

She nodded. "Or pick the light blue one. I think they also have souvenir ties there too. Did you use up your ship credits?

"Nooo," replied Randy. He'd forgotten about that.

"Then it shouldn't cost you much. I only had to chip in a little to cover for my hairstylist."

"Excuse me." It was the elderly lady.

Randy glanced over his shoulder. *She had to be at least two hundred pounds.* The woman had already turned sideways to edge her way past them and the housekeeping cart. *Nowhere to go but forward,* concluded Randy. Ashley had drawn the same conclusion. She'd dropped her hands to her side as Randy leaned into her.

It wasn't the old lady squeezing by that captured Randy's attention. It was the body heat from Ashley as he drew closer. It was all he could do to resist putting his arms around her and drawing her tight against himself. That resistance was short-lived.

"Excuse me." That was the old man.

He's even larger, observed Randy. *Ashley's back will be wedged into the corner of the doorframe. That could hurt.* Randy's arms reached behind Ashley's back and drew her in as the old fellow began to pass by. He hardly noticed the slight pain in his lower arm as they were pressed firmly into the doorframe. It was Ashley's breasts first touching, then melting against his chest that held his attention. There were so many times in the past few days he'd hoped to just hold her in his arms, but she never allowed him to get that close.

Ashley's throat clearing betrayed the fact that he'd attempted to prolong this moment too long. Slowly, the upper half of Randy's body bent back, reducing the pressure of the doorframe against his arms. He looked down. Ashley was staring straight ahead, as if she were in a trance. His hand moved softly up and down her back, coming to rest just above her hip. After a moment, his hand applied a slight pressure, as if they were dancing. "You sure you couldn't spare a few minutes?" he whispered softly in her ear. Silence. *No swift expected rejection. She's considering it.* He was certain. "In your cabin," he added, his hope growing with every second of silence.

As Randy leaned against her, Ashley lost touch with reality. She slipped back a few years to the time after class when Brian, Queen Elizabeth's grade-twelve high school running back, had snagged her arm as she strolled past the caretaker's storage room. At first, she protested being pulled into the room. His assurance of "Don't worry, Hasberg'll be gone for a while," resulted in the storage room door being closed behind her. The boy, whom she'd flirted with for the last couple of months, finally made his feelings known. A taste of heaven engulfed her when his arms gently wrapped around her. *Treasured and adored above all else—there's nothing like it.* Only the closet wall against her back seemed real. When he leaned back, still pinning her against the wall, she looked up, straight into his shining eyes. He'd waited until she initiated their first kiss.

Recovery slowly began. The present asserted itself. Ashley felt the sensation of a hand slightly pressuring her lower back. *I'm being hugged!* The body warmth was certain, a male's excitement, undeniable. Fear of what was actually happening temporarily froze Ashley. Desperate for clarity, she looked up. Pain shot into her neck and then flooded the entire back of her head. Her leg muscles lost all strength. Darkness descended. The floor began to absorb her. The past reclaimed Ashley's memory.

Like an avalanche, Ashley relived flying through the air, crashing to the living room floor, banging her head. *How was it possible that Brian, then her loving husband of two years, had slugged her! Why was he raging like a madman?* He'd had mood swings, but nothing that hinted on death at the doorstep. Divorce delayed, anger management course, restraining orders, divorce finalized all flashed through Ashley's mind like strikes of lightning.

"Ashley, Ashley, you all right? Say something," urged a shocked and worried Randy. The fog of Ashley's past began to dissipate.

"Brian?" mumbled Ashley uncertainly.

"It's Randy, Ashley. You all right? Should I call a doctor?"

Like a light switch being turned on in the early morning, the name Randy triggered her memory: *Eurodam* cruise, outside cabin 4025. Doctor meant endless embarrassing explanations. Fighting to regain her previous composure, she strongly asserted, "No doctor, please. Just help me inside. I'll be fine in a while."

With Ashley safely propped against her cabin door, Randy poked his hand in the Holland America bag, felt for Ashley's paperback, and pulled it out. Dog-earring the page where her cabin card was in case it served as a bookmarker, he reached around Ashley and inserted the card. A little green light flashed rapidly. Randy turned the handle and pushed the door open. Ashley shuffled into her cabin, carefully feeling her way along the wall. Randy followed close beside her without touching her. With her arm stretched before her, Ashley slowly leaned forward toward her bed and then sat down.

Seeing her finally relax a little, Randy knelt down in front of her. He looked up into her face. "Ashley, what happened out there?"

This wasn't the first time Ashley hid the truth. "An old injury, a whiplash that comes back to haunt me sometimes when I make a wrong move."

"You sure you'll be fine? You know you don't have to go to the dinner if you do not want to."

Ashley appreciated his concern. "I *want to* go to the dinner. I'll be fine. Could you go to the washroom and bring me the Tylenol and a bottle of water? The pills are sitting in the cabinet above the sink." In a few moments, he returned.

"If there's anything else I can do, you know I'm just at the end of the corridor." Randy didn't want leave, but he didn't know what else could be done.

"Do your shopping," Ashley urged, hoping that would signal that she was already on the mend. "Maybe come back and check on me about four thirty. I don't want to be late for my hair appointment." She suspected lying down on the bed might cause her to oversleep, especially after taking the medication. With a nod, Randy heeded her request. The cabin door closed, and Ashley put her head on the pillow and stretched a comforter over herself. *Even in the Mediterranean, even after four years of no contact, Brian's berserk behavior continues to haunt me. Would it ever disappear?*

To drown her former husband's unexpected explosive behavior from her mind, Ashley turned to recent encounters with Randy. In the preceding five days, their paths crossed many times. Even the first cruise day on a ship of about 1,900 people, their chance meetings felt oddly coincidental.

Their first encounter occurred at seven fifteen in the morning. During Ashley's brisk walk on the promenade deck, a pair of black-and-white soccer shorts sporting the Edmonton Ruffians breezed by. Brian had taken her to a few of Ruffian games. After the surprisingly tanned jogger passed her for the third time, she made a point of actually seeing who was in such fine shape. He breathed easily as he effortlessly passed by her again. *I can't even jog one lap around the ship*, she confessed to herself. *Very short brownish hair, tuned into something on his iPod*, she noted. His white T-shirt was neatly tucked into his jogging shorts. She reached the deck door near her cabin.

A quick shower and breakfast on the Lido deck meant she was a little early for her first excursion. The four-hour tour took her to the Leaning Tower of Pisa and some beautiful huge cathedrals. Back on the ship while still recalling the breathtaking detailed paintings and sculptures in the cathedrals, she spotted Randy awkwardly playing in some shipboard table tennis match. *He's not very good*, she concluded. She continued exploring deck 3.

Then that same evening, Randy joined her at the dinner table. After the first evening of sitting at a dinner table with no one she knew, Ashley asked the maître d' if he could place her at a table with some Albertans. She was lucky. A table seating eight had an elderly couple from an acreage near Spruce Grove and two middle-aged couples from the west side of Edmonton. After their introductions, conversations about West Edmonton Mall and the Oilers struggling for a play-off position, she felt comfortable. It was like being on a coffee break back at the bank.

"Pardon me. You people from around Edmonton?" Randy asked, interrupting Mrs. Wassel as she lamented the poor goaltending of the Oilers. Randy was in the process of being escorted to a seat at some other table. Mr. Wassel's affirmative answer grew a huge smile on Randy's face. "Hey, I'm from Sherwood Park and . . ." He paused, debating if he should risk exposing himself as a loner, but their smiles encouraged him. "I have to confess I'm on the cruise alone." Pointing to the empty chair by Ashley, he continued, "I'd sure love to join you if that seat isn't taken." Randy noted the smiles and nods from everyone around the table except Ashley, but she hadn't objected either. He waved the waiter off and sat down beside her.

"My name's Randy Watson. Among other things, I'm a sports manager. A little over a week ago, I came to Barcelona to register our soccer rep team for summer training. I spent the rest of the time exploring Barcelona to see what other kinds of activities I might be able to introduce our players to. I figured, while I'm down here, I might as well take in a tour or a cruise."

Randy had set the stage for introductions. Harriet and John Wassel said they were from a small acreage just south of Spruce Grove. John was a retired used-vehicle salesman from Fuhr Ford Mercury. Dick Cordeck introduced himself as a printer at World Color Printers and his wife, Jean, as a salesclerk at Sears in West Edmonton Mall. George Reynolds worked for Promotions Inc., a firm that designed advertising campaigns. It broke off from World Color Printers when they reorganized. Brenda, his wife, was with the same advertising company. She designed layouts for flyers. Their printing was often sent to World Color Printers.

"Ashley Norris. I work at the TD bank in the Northtown Mall." She didn't intend to give too much information to this table of strangers.

"So you all know each other?" queried Randy. He learned that the three couples were also members of the same United Church. Ashley was not mentioned as being a part of that group. A slight smile flashed across his face. Ashley rightly suspected Randy was pleased to know that she was alone like he was.

"I can't tell you how happy I am to find people from Edmonton," Randy offered cheerfully. "I was afraid I wouldn't know a soul."

"Listen, we don't have assigned seating, but you two are welcome to join us for the rest of the cruise. All you have to do is reserve a seat at table 85. That's this table," Harriet offered. "You can only reserve three days in advance, but so long as you keep renewing it, we will be together."

"How do I reserve?" asked Randy.

"Just see the maître d' when you leave."

"Sounds great. What do you think?" asked Randy, looking at Ashley.

She loved the idea of joining the Albertans again. *Why doesn't Randy just say he'd do it? Why ask me? He doesn't need my permission.* "Thanks for the invitation. I'd love to accept," responded Ashley.

"Good!" exclaimed Randy. "We'll do it right after supper."

We? noted Ashley. *Kind of presumptuous.*

When everyone had selected the choices for the four-course meal, Randy turned to Ashley and asked her how it was that she had taken the cruise alone. "I was supposed to be going with two other friends, Danielle and Carol," Ashley explained. "We all still had last year's holidays to finish off. Before work started, I saw on the web a fantastic Holland America last-minute deal. They had a 40 percent discount with a hundred-dollar ship credit for this cruise. At our Friday morning coffee break, I told my friends about it. We all agreed to go. I booked my passage right after the break. What I didn't know is that they had been immediately called in for some special meeting. It had taken them through their lunch hour. By the time they phoned in the afternoon, the remaining cabins were taken. I hadn't heard they missed their booking until Monday morning coffee. By then, it seemed too late to cancel, so I decided to go. I'd always wanted to come to the Mediterranean anyway." After the meal, Ashley and Randy together reserved their next three suppers for table 85.

The following morning, Saturday, Ashley saw Randy jogging again. He didn't appear to have noticed her. Her hair was done up, unlike last night. They both were on the half-day "Highlight of Monaco and Monte Carlo" tour. The moment he saw her on the bus, a smile radiated from his face. He approached and asked, "May I join you?" He was among the last to board the bus. There weren't many other seats available. As expected, she granted him his request.

They had laughed and talked all morning. *How well we connected! He's so in tune with me. It's as if we'd been hanging around together for a year.* Near the end of the excursion, Ashley became aware that she ceased to be of equal importance with the sites.

They'd wound their way up a narrow road to a luxurious huge casino. The tour guide offered this little something extra. The last museum closed a substantial part of its place for unexpected maintenance. An opportunity to visit a high-end gambling establishment was a greatly appreciated bonus. Randy's star attraction was a small VIP parking lot of no more than twenty "dream cars". The new Rolls-Royce, Jaguars, Lamborghinis, and Porsches held him captive for at least half an hour. He talked to the guard about the cars, their owners, and his job until it was almost time to leave. Ashley joined the other tourists in exploring the casino interior.

For almost half the trip back to the ship, stories Randy picked up from the outside attendant kept popping out of him. "Can you imagine? One of the owners tipped him a *grand* for watching over his vehicle! 'You gotta love big winners,' the guard had proclaimed joyfully." Even after he'd returned to the ship and was waiting his turn to play a second table tennis match, his car lot stories spilled into the conversations. Of course, when he played, his mind had a single focus: the game. It didn't matter. He still lost.

Oooh, Barcelona! recalled Ashley. She'd already paid for "A Taste of Barcelona," another four-hour excursion. Randy couldn't convince her to drop it in favor of him showing her around the place in which he'd spent a week, so he committed to joining her on the tour, if she'd stay with him after.

"There are so many wonderful things to see and do," he proclaimed. "You have to let me show you some of the sites I found." When that sales pitch didn't work, Randy altered strategies. "You'd be doing me a favor if you let me show you around." Her surprised look told him he had her. "Really. It'll be good practice for me. I'll be better able to show the soccer rep team around when they're here in the summer." She was weakening. "I'll have you back at the ship on time." She shook her head. That wasn't her concern. "You'll have a great time. If not, I'll . . . I'll . . ." He desperately searched for a compensating offer. "I'll take you to supper at the captain's table."

Ashley laughed. "How do you think you'll manage that?" she asked, puzzled about such an unusual offer.

She was hooked. "By winning the next table tennis match tomorrow," he announced confidently. Even before she finished groaning her disbelief, he proclaimed, "You've no idea what I can do when I set my mind to it."

"I'm beginning to," she responded with a laugh.

"Well?" he persisted.

Suspecting he might resort to begging next, she agreed. "How can I lose?"

"Exactly!"

The Barcelona bus tour was like the last one. The minibus took them to the Gothic quarter and the exterior of several huge cathedrals. Sunday meant tourists couldn't interrupt the services. After many picture-snapping opportunities, they were deposited in a tourist shopping center.

Randy slipped a few euros to the minivan driver for a five-minute ride to the tourist info center, next to the oldest part of Barcelona. Here, they rented bikes, a programmed iPod, and a city center map with historic sites coded on the map, which could be entered on the iPod for a brief historical description. The hour-and-a-half activity took over two hours because they stopped for lunch and later some must-try pastry.

Knowing Ashley's interest in art, from overhearing a part of Ashley's conversation with Harriet Wassel, Randy took her to an art museum that was a block and a half from the info center. To her surprise, it featured over a hundred works of Picasso's art. A half-hour video reviewed his life and work. Just when Ashley thought the day was perfect, Randy paid for a horse-carriage ride through the historic center. *It doesn't get any better than a relaxing ride with a heavy, warm quilt on your lap and a personal guide explaining everything you saw. Clearly, Randy had studied up on this tourist attraction to impress his young soccer players.* The driver even went a little out of his way and dropped them off at the info center, where they caught a cab back to the ship. They returned half an hour before the ship left port.

Ashley's mini scrap book

Forum tower and Water Tower

Water Tower Preserved

Modern Transportation and Past Transportation

Agbar Torpedo and Christopher Columbus

Sagrada Familia and Restoration Effort

On Monday, the ship docked at Valencia, Spain. After their early-morning workout on the promenade deck, they enjoyed breakfast together on the Lido deck. Ashley took the "City of Porcelain" tour to Lladro a porcelain arts center. Randy took a different excursion.

That same afternoon, while the ship was still in port, Ashley found Randy in the games area, on the eighth deck, among a dozen or so other men surrounding a pool table. The last winner, a tall slender fellow called Todd, challenged his spectators. "Eight ball, anyone?" When no one stepped up, Randy volunteered. It was the cheering that pulled Ashley's attention to the table.

"Gotta ten?" asked Todd as he walked over to the cue rack and plucked some bills wrapped around a cue stick. He waved a ten euro and placed it around one of the remaining cue sticks. "Makes the game a little more interesting," he urged. Randy glanced at the audience. The request didn't seem unexpected to them. He fished the money out of his wallet and placed it with Todd's.

Todd broke. No ball fell. Randy's first shot was an easy straight-in shot to the corner pocket. The challenge he chose for his second shot required his solid ball to just slide by two striped balls and drop in the side pocket. It would draw a murmur of approval if he succeeded. Instead, he miscued, and the white ball just touched the target. Snickers from a couple of Todd's travelling companions drowned out the few sympathizing ahhhs.

"Todd," called one of his buddies. "This will be like taking candy from a baby. Put a little pressure on yourself. Bump the odds to three to one." Todd looked at his two laughing buddies, then took a twenty from his last winnings, and placed it with the two tens.

"No problem," he retorted and began shooting, calling his shots. He dropped five striped balls in a row with nods of approval from the audience.

"Good shooting," complimented Randy as he sized up the table. Ashley began to leave. "Hang on, Ashley. This'll be over in a few minutes." Ashley looked back and nodded, indicating she'd wait.

"Now just reeeelaaaax. Take it easy," encouraged Matt, one of Todd's friends. He smiled broadly at Randy.

Randy smiled back. He had enjoyed teasing players in the past too. With one final glance at Ashley to confirm that she was still watching, he chalked his cue and turned his attention back to the table. With slow deliberate strokes, he pocketed his next six balls. Silence around the table was in respect of his concentrated play. Only his last shot was challenging. It required a firm stroke with a good spin on the cue ball to put him in position for a straightforward shot on the eight ball. It would have to travel almost all the way across the table to drop in the corner pocket. He paused, chalked his cue stick, and enjoyed the tension on Todd's face. If this ball didn't drop, there was no doubt that Todd would finish him off. Then with the same ease as he demonstrated on his previous shots, Randy sent the eight ball racing to the corner pocket. Loud cheering proclaimed his success. Randy looked up to see Ashley was among the most enthusiastic about his win. He returned the cue stick to the rack and claimed his winnings.

As he turned to join Ashley, Randy felt a hand pull his arm back. "Hey, aren't you going to give me a chance to get my money back?"

"Sorry," Randy responded coolly. "My girl is ready to leave." He looked at Ashley. She was already glancing at her watch.

"I've been set up," objected Todd loudly.

"If that's the case, it was by your own friends," replied Randy. The strain on Todd's face didn't change. "Look," added Randy after a moment of silence, "I was happy to play the game for fun. I don't need your money. Here, you can have it back." He tossed Todd's thirty euros on the table.

Matt walked swiftly from his end of the table and picked up the money. He shoved it back in Randy's hand. "This is yours. You won it fair and square. Don't mind Todd. He's just being a sore loser." Matt glared straight into his friend's face. Todd nodded in agreement and looked down.

The group around the table began to break up. Randy joined Ashley, putting his arm around her waist. She slipped it off.

"My girl?" she quoted questioningly. *This is the second time he's laid a claim on me. I haven't agreed to anything. He needs to know that we're just friends, friends for the cruise.*

"Oh, that. It was just an easy way of getting out of another game," he said, smiling at how clever he thought he was. The fact that it hadn't worked on Todd was irrelevant. It tested Ashley's response.

New opportunities for Randy and Ashley to be together arose. That evening, they attended their first after-dinner show, featuring comedian Lee Bayless. Using his Midwest U.S. background, he highlighted the *Eurodam*'s oddities for unsuspecting first-time cruisers. His references to backward-turning bathroom taps and the four-inch-raised bathroom floors that tripped half-asleep nighttime visitors had the audience roaring. Then there was his joy at being on the *Eurodam* instead of the *Noordam*, especially if the *Noordam* should encounter rough seas. The *Eurodam* had their lifeboats on board.

The after-dinner show won their hearts. The invitation to come the next day to hear comedian ventriloquist Phil Hughes and the following day's award-winning pianist, Vladimir Zaitsev, easily received confirmation nods from Randy and Ashley. Concluding the evening with a visit to the Crow's Nest for a drink or two, some singing and dancing created a treasured memory.

Once again, the next day, Ashley suspected Lady Luck was playing Cupid. The Modernist Art and Architecture tour in San Antonio was undersubscribed. It was canceled at the last minute. Secretly, Ashley was pleased. *My souvenir spending, leather purse, shoes, and shawl are more than I expected. The cruise is just half over. The refund on the excursion will be credited to my account and will balance out my spending.*

The tour director was in the process of suggesting alternative options when Randy arrived. "Anything close by where we can just wander around and absorb the flavor of San Antonio? You know, close enough that we could hire a cab for?" Randy asked.

"Modernist Art and Architecture?" asked Ashley, a little surprised. Randy nodded.

The tour director's face brightened. "You might like this," she said, looking at Ashley. "There's a beach not too far away from here where they have great little shops and restaurants. In the open square, there are several artists painting and sketching. You might even get a portrait of yourself."

It was midmorning when they left the ship. Ashley and Randy split the cab cost. She insisted. They wandered through narrow winding street malls. Around noon, they sat in the shade by the open square, enjoying a Sprite and some fresh pastry. It was then Randy confessed he was pleased the modern art tour was canceled too. He admitted switching from a wine-tasting excursion to the art tour when he learned what Ashley had signed up for.

The expression on her face caused Randy to reach over, place a finger under her chin, and gently lift it up. As he started to explain how he hoped to recapture the Barcelona atmosphere, a tall young guy in short ragged jeans interrupted them. His black hair was scattered on the top of his head like it had never seen a comb. In his left hand, he had a large pad of paper. Through a combination of Spanish and English, he indicated he wanted to draw a picture of Ashley.

She shook her head. *He'll expect me to buy it then. Who knows how good it will be? When he's completed his work, how can one then refuse? Best to say no even before he starts. This is supposed to be a low-expense day.* After shaking her head for the third time, she gave up. Randy and the artist won.

For the next fifteen minutes, Randy and Ashley sat talking at the little round plastic table, enjoying a second piece of pastry. Randy entertained Ashley by recalling the time they spent together in Barcelona. Ashley's smiles told him she felt the same way he did, even though she never said so.

The young artist, who stood about ten paces away from their table in the hot sun, busily motored his right hand over the paper pad that was pressed into his hip. His head frequently twitched from the pad, briefly to his subjects, and returned. As his work neared completion, he smiled and sought little details to even more clearly capture the moment. The hand movements slowed. A crowd of spectators slowly gathered behind him, watching the performance. After a thoughtful pause, he scribbled his name on the bottom right-hand corner of the pad and approached the table. He placed his pad between them so they could both admire the picture.

There was Ashley, her head propped on her upright-folded hands. Her head, leaning slightly right and back, looked happily at her companion across the table. The smiling eyes and partially opened mouth held Randy's attention. The brown bangs arched away from the top of her head and came back to gently rest just above her darkened eyebrows. The thick ponytail appeared to suspend far enough away from her head so it could easily bounce right and left as it had when Ashley momentarily peeked at the working artist. The right edge of the paper caught a bit of Randy's profile too.

The audience followed the young man. Had he found a patron? After giving them a few minutes to admire his work, the artist turned salesman. He took the pad back, tore the picture free, and placed it in front of Randy.

Ashley relaxed as she watched Randy deliberating. *The problem is Randy's. How is he going to turn this guy down now, especially with a crowd of admirers?*

He looked up at the fellow. "How much?"

Randy's buying it! I don't believe it. Ashley looked at the artist, hoping he'd announce an outrageously high price so Randy could turn it down. The young man held out his open hand. It was Randy's choice. *Now he's trapped.* Ashley felt sorry for Randy.

Randy took his wallet out and briefly examined its contents: a five, some twenties, and a few fifties. He pulled out a twenty-euro bill, looked up at the artist, and held it out. The smile on the artist's face sealed the deal. A few spectators applauded.

After they were alone again, Ashley leaned forward. "You realize . . ." She paused. "You were set up."

"I don't know. I think he just did me a favor."

"What do you mean?"

"He captured you perfectly. This is you when I was telling you about our time in Barcelona. What better way to recapture that moment in time than by having a picture of us reliving it! There's only one thing missing."

"What?"

He slid the picture over to her. "Your name on the back."

"Pardon me?"

He flipped the portrait facedown on the table. "Why don't you write . . ." He paused, as if figuring out what he wanted on the back. "From Ashley to Randy," he said with a huge grin.

"You're kidding?" She searched for his hidden motivation. *We don't have that kind of relationship.*

"Ahh, come on," he persisted. "You kindly posed for the work."

"And that's more than enough."

"Okay, then just write, 'of Ashley.'"

"You write it." As he reached out to slide the portrait back to himself, Ashley had an idea. "Wait a minute." She fished in her little clutch purse for a pen. Then at the bottom right-hand corner on the back, she wrote, "the holiday girl, Ashley." *Maybe that'll clue him in. Our relationship is just holiday friends.*

He looked at what she wrote, smiled, and rolled up the portrait. Together they walked out to the beach. With their sandals off, they enjoyed the warm sand squeezing in between their toes until they were stopped by a shout, "Randy!" Looking around, they recognized Ronda and Jeff, a married couple a little older than they were. They were on the *Eurodam* cruise too. With them were their fellow Denver, Colorado, friends. All four of them excitedly waved Randy and Ashley over. As they neared their shipmates, Jeff invited them to join the four of them. He pointed to several local young people standing near a volleyball net looking in their direction. "Tourists take on the locals?"

Randy eagerly accepted, then looked at Ashley for her reaction. She was in. He pulled his T-shirt off, setting it on the nearby bench. After inserting each end of the portrait in a sandal, he sized up their opponents, both girls and guys, all in their late teens or early twenties. *They'd have energy on their side. Probably have played together too*, Randy concluded. It didn't matter. It was the game, the plays. That would make the afternoon fun.

The first game the tourists lost big-time, but the second game, they only lost by three points. The Cruisers, the name they gave themselves, were just learning how to play as a team. Jeff, athletically minded like Randy, thrived upon competition. He loudly promoted a positive spirit. Al, Jeff's friend, played well but just didn't have the drive or the heart to make that little extra effort to get to the ball. Mandy, Al's wife, understood the game well. Several times, she made it appear as if there was a hole on the Cruisers' side, only to prove that she was just waiting for the server to be sucked in. She'd step up with well-placed returns. Rhonda and Ashley laughed continually whether their shots made it over the net or not. The confidence arising from the second game enabled the Cruisers to accept a challenge—losers buy the sangria. Once again, the third game was close. The Cruisers bought the sangria at the beach bar.

The party atmosphere lasted for about an hour. The locals spoke excellent English. Randy exchanged e-mail addresses with several of them. Tentative plans were for them to come to Barcelona when Randy's soccer rep team was there in the summer.

Then Randy announced that he had to be back at the ship. He had a four o'clock table tennis match to win. Carlos and Jordi volunteered to drive the Cruisers back to their ship. "A consolation prize," they said.

"One of the best onshore days I've had!" announced Randy as he tucked his rolled portrait under his arm.

Ashley agreed. *If only I can limit Randy's expectations of me.*

They arrived about ten minutes early for the third and last scheduled table tennis match. Randy's cheering section, the Cruisers, was prepared to support his every effort. Each of the eight players had deposited a ten-euro entry fee that served as a donation for the Save the Children Fund. The contest began with two sets of doubles playing. The winners from the two doubles matches then played each other. Finally, the winners of the last doubles match played each other. This last stage was a best of three matches. As before, Randy made it to this level. After winning his first singles match by a five-point spread, he looked at Ashley and gave her a wink as if to say the next game was his too. Ashley smiled back. She understood the "See what I can do when I set my mind to it?" message. Randy's heightened motivation and cheering section were too much for his opponent. Randy won with a five-point margin. Ashley screamed and jumped for joy and threw her arms around her dinner-winning hero. Randy's smile took over his whole face. It proclaimed he'd won the game, the dinner, and the girl.

Ashley's thoughts turned to the present. *And now, today, it was almost a perfect sea day, a day to tan and read. The incident in the hall just outside my cabin door when Randy had me pinned against the doorframe shouldn't have happened. He really wanted me to let him into my cabin. Those hands sliding up and down my back were itching to reach down and find the tie string on my bikini. I even caught myself momentarily wishing we were inside. When I was looking up to shake my head if he'd tried to kiss me . . . I don't know. This is all happening too fast.*

Knock, knock, knock. The cabin ceiling came into sharp focus. A stiff neck dragged Ashley into the present. *Knock, knock, knock.*

The door, concluded Ashley as she slipped the Holland America comforter off.

Sliding her hand along the cabin wall, she steadied herself on the way to the peephole in the cabin door. *Randy! What's he doing here?*

She opened the door and stepped back. She hazily recalled asking Randy to come back later.

"Hey, I know I'm a little early, but—"

"What time is it?'

"About four twenty. I wanted to see if you're all right and show you what I bought." Ashley saw the white Holland America bag held in Randy's left hand.

"I'm kind of okay. I just lost track of time. Thanks for coming so early." As Randy prepared to take out his purchase, Ashley interrupted him. "I don't mean to sound rude or anything, but I haven't showered yet, so I'll have to ask you to excuse me."

Randy slid his purchase back into the bag. "No problem. May I come and escort you to dinner, say about six forty-five?" With a nod from Ashley, Randy left.

While Ashley's hair dried, Stella, her stylist, left to serve other clients. *Finally,* Ashley thought with a sigh. *Now maybe I can sort out what's really bothering me this afternoon. I wish I could say it's Randy's growing interest in me. I just wish I could get him to back off. I don't want to be rude about it. No, actually, I think I really don't want to completely put a stop to his attention. He's made this holiday exciting and more fun than I thought possible.*

She looked at the book she brought to read. The edge of her special blue bookmark peeked out. *If only you'd fallen out so Randy could have picked you up,* she wished. She opened her book, extracted the marker, and read Adam's poem, "A Candy to Catch"—the poem she had asked Adam to give to her before she went on the cruise.

A Candy to Catch

The concrete sugary savoring
stimulated by a sight, a taste, a promise
may steal a child's safety
drawing them in like a magnet--
"Don't, take candy from a stranger."

Still, the adult child savors
the sweetness of a smile
generous compliments, a favor or two
sometimes softening safety senses too--
"Don't, take candy from a stranger."

Safer sweetness to savor
stretches over time with someone.
A trust relationship is the concrete sugar.

by Adam Aski

Then like cold water from the morning tap splashing over her face, the complexity of her dilemma hit. *It's all there—in the poem, on the bookmark.* Adam was the first guy she really let be close to her since her divorce. *Brian was once that sweet candy. Now it's Randy. He's the same kind of unknown sweet candy. Randy's not the candy to catch. Adam is. Adam I can trust.*

"Adam, I wish you were here now," she whispered. She wanted to hear her wish as if she were finally letting out a secret, as if saying it out loud would make it happen. At the same time, she knew it was impossible. This was the busiest part of the year for an accountant.

Holding Adam's bookmark close to her heart, Ashley recalled the promise she made to herself after finally feeling that she was rid of Brian: *never be involved with another man again.* Then over two years, Ashley slowly accepted Adam's attention. Adam, a regular client at the TD bank, frequently appeared at her business wicket. Their usual social chatter grew more personal over time, at least on Adam's part.

One day, Adam had shared an unusual personal problem. He had, from a very grateful client, a complimentary pass to the Mayfield Dinner Theatre. No one in Adam's office was available to go with him. They were busy, married, or going out with someone. "It's the third time I've had to return Mayfield dinner tickets to the client or just let it go unused. He's been really disappointed when I turn down his kind offers," complained Adam.

"Ahh, no one to go out with for a free dinner," laughed Ashley, trying to lighten the mood. "Such a hard problem to solve." Her humor didn't work. He'd even looked hurt. Ashley felt the need to apologize.

"You don't believe me!" He paused. "Let me show you. Are you presently attached to a guy?" She shook her head. "Would you like to go out with me to the Mayfield Dinner Theatre this Saturday?"

Her first inclination was to come up with some excuse. The truth was she had no plans. She'd heard the show was good, and she always felt comfortable talking with Adam when he came to her wicket. *Once can't hurt*, she recalled rationalizing. *It wasn't like it was costing him anything.* If he had paid for it, she'd have felt obligated to share the expense. There was no way she was going to be in a guy's debt. To his surprise, she accepted.

In the two hours they had to eat their dinner before the show, Ashley discovered she and Adam had many common interests. Like her, he loved reading, and he loved kids. Every month and sometimes twice, he read to the kids in the St. Albert Public Library to promote reading. He loved dramatizing many parts from books to really excite the kids. Adam claimed it was part of his responsibility as a member of the local writer's club that used the library every other Tuesday. His eagerness for sharing stories with the kids impressed Ashley. She remembered she used to be one of those kids.

Adam also helped supervise the Young People's corn maze events at the United Church, the same church she attended. She'd never even seen him there, although she wasn't a regular attendee. His love of art, festivals, and folk music enabled him to make excellent connections with his clients. They were also responsible for the many complimentary passes he told her he received.

Over the following months, Ashley found herself enjoying many more of Adam's complimentary passes. When Adam confessed he'd created some of the "complimentary" passes just so he could be out with Ashley, she was surprised that she wasn't annoyed. Her promise to not let another guy buy their way into her favor was slipping. Her awareness of it didn't bother her either.

One evening, on the way back to St. Albert, Adam stopped in at the Castle Downs Boston Pizza. They'd spent the whole weekend at the Fringe and would still have been there if the line for the last play hadn't been so long. Leaving a little early meant fewer people in the restaurant so they could sit and talk in relative privacy. *Adam must have planned for that because after our order was placed, he pulled a poem out of his shirt pocket: "Note to Self . . . for . . ."* He told her he'd written it for himself a few weeks before he had asked her to go out on their first Mayfield dinner. Writing it gave him the courage to ask her out.

Note to Self . . . for . . .

Extend yourself
to another
without lifting a hand.
A smile
warms,
draws the other
nearer
warming you too.

Extend yourself,
praise the other
in other's presence,
in the other's presence
and so be praised.

Extend yourself,
offer a helping hand
here and there
now and then
as opportunity
not need
presents.
A precious treasure
to be guarded
you can be.
Extend yourself

being a quiet, calm, gentle power
as a match flame
waiting,
ready
to light a candle,
a lantern
to give birth to a campfire
for fellowship time
for security.

You can be
potential power prepared
to reach out
in service.

Extend yourself
seeing silver lining
through cloud stealing sun; and
polishing
tarnished tools
draws out the other's
hidden brilliance—
points a way out.
You, sign of hope,
save the other
from a day of sorrow.

Yourself extended
a smile warming, being warmed
enhancing, enhanced
an offering at anytime
a can do power on hand,
a hope generator, are treasured

                    by A d a m A s k i

"If you would have laughed at me or turned me down, I would have considered changing branches," Ashley recalled him confessing.

Asking me to go out scared him. I hadn't thought this extrovert was so vulnerable. Ashley had hid her surprise.

As he read his poem to me, I pictured him following the advice he'd given himself. I was surprised at Adam's eagerness and him hoping to develop a friendship with me. I'd never indicated anything other than a business connection. That was all I wanted. Yet after a little less than half a year, he began revealing personal feelings, secrets I wouldn't have dared to reveal to anyone so soon. How he could develop such a trust in me so fast, I didn't know! At first, I thought he was foolish.

When he'd finished reading his poem, I told him that I was flattered by his interest in me and impressed by his courage to take a chance that he would be rejected. Now that I think back on it, I suspect that he meant that poem for me too. He wanted me to extend myself, to reach out to him. I should have suspected as much when he asked me what was wrong.

I was caught totally off guard. I hadn't said anything or done anything to indicate I was angry or annoyed. I almost froze to the chair. Could he see inside me, see my most private thoughts? It was almost as if my blouse was unbuttoned.

"I shared some very personal parts of my life. I felt like I could really trust you. You've listened with a very compassionate heart as I thought you would." He'd taken a breath to continue but then took a long pause. "You've said very little about yourself. I don't mean about your work. I mean about who you are. For a while, I wondered if you didn't trust me.

"Then I suspected that someone had really hurt you, and you were afraid to trust anyone. I recalled how sometimes you jumped when I touched your elbow or suddenly jerked your hand away when I reached back for your arm so we would stick together in a crowd. There was even once I had put my arm around your shoulder and you looked at me so fast with such narrow piercing eyes I thought I'd done something really wrong. I imagined you were about to slap my face."

His observations, his spoken insight hurt. He knew I wasn't the self-assured person he thought I was.

"I know that reluctance to reveal yourself to someone else. You see, I've been afraid to strike up any kind of a personal relationship with another girl. For almost six years, including all our high school years, Sherry and I went out together, did everything together. I thought—even my friends thought—sometime after graduation, we'd get married.

"Then midway through my first semester of university, she quit seeing me, quit phoning me, quit texting me. When I asked what was wrong, she said nothing was wrong. She just had other interests she wanted to pursue. It had nothing to do with me. Just like that! Right out of the blue! I never saw it coming! I was devastated. My honor marks dropped.

"I almost failed my first year. Darryl, my high school buddy who also registered in the business faculty, saw I was in trouble. We talked. Then he called Barb, his older sister. We were all fairly close. She'd convinced me that I needed to focus on my studies to save my year, that Sherry was just one part of my life.

"For a while, I was able to bury myself in my studies and then my new job. I even became involved in some church events to distract me."

Ashley recalled being so caught up in Adam's revelation that she had momentarily forgotten her own embarrassment. "And so you haven't dated since then?" she concluded.

"Not until you went out with me to the Mayfield," he confessed. In a lowered voice, he continued, "You don't think I'm some kind of a weirdo, do you?"

Ashley had shaken her head. She knew that Adam was right about her. Ashley knew that fear all too well. Even after his revelation, she couldn't tell Adam about her failed marriage. *I felt incapable of judging men. I was even afraid of a deeper relationship with Adam.*

"I was sure if I told you about how poorly I handled my breakup with Sherry, you'd think I was weird. You'd find a way to quit going out with me. I worried about it so much I finally put my feelings into a poem." He took a second folded sheet of paper from his pocket. "And don't read it now," he said before giving it to her. "I just wanted you to know that I think so much of you that I would never do anything to upset you. And . . ." He paused, worried he might seem like he was pushing her too hard. "If your past experience is too painful to share, I will live with it, although I would really like to share that burden with you if you'd let me."

That night, before Ashley slipped out of Adam's car, he explained that he used a different girl's name in the poem because he thought she might not like it if he used hers. It was almost a reminder to read his poem after he left. She did. Just before she went to bed, she read "Jill, a Beauty to Behold." *Adam's experience with Sherry haunted him throughout the poem. How in the world did he see me as such a resolute person! He's wrong there. Once he really gets to know me, he will be disappointed.* Still, she had to admit it felt good to be seen as such a strong person. *He too sees himself as fairly strong-willed.* She fell asleep with several of his phrases rattling around in her head: "a rose," "miracle in progress," "overlooked gem," "don't touch," "I will," "flowering glory."

Jill, A Beauty to Behold

A rose just within an arm's reach
bordered by shiny, black, iron railing bars
nestled between three granite boulders
struggling for life in shallow soil
attempting to grow to the stature of bushy roses all around
a seemingly, discarded rose
deliberately deposited, to be unseen
from a grand old house 50 yards away

and yet many thin branches with tiny green leaves
beckon,
from rough, dark, dry bark
defiantly proclaiming
I am NOT to be discounted.
Clustered, uncared for growth
foretells of the beauty of the surrounding cousins and
surprised praise, to come when tiny blossoms unfold their brilliance alone
spotlighting a spirit that should not have been untended.

I am drawn
to look in from the outside
to supplement the sun's warmth, and the rain's caress
perhaps by begging the distant gardener for
        a sprinkling of fertilizer
        a loosening of the soil
an acknowledgement of a miracle in progress.
To confirm the reality of such an overlooked gem and
to be like an encouraging pat on the back
        a light, little finger-tip touch-attempt
brings a thorn piercing, a scratching.
Don't touch! Leave me alone.
I WILL
live.

Such proud persistent strength!
I must return
to assure no harm disturbs
her unexpected
flowering glory.

By A d a m A s k i

It took almost two weeks after Adam had given Ashley his poem for him to dare to show up at the TD bank. Depositing one of his client's checks was the excuse he needed. It was a chance to see how Ashley would react to his presence. She hadn't called or anything. Adam was very much afraid he'd lost her. That fear vanished the moment he stepped into the bank. Ashley looked up from the wicket, waved, and turned on a huge smile. No one else was at the wicket. Adam looked behind him as he walked up the business lane. He smiled; no one else was following him. They could talk.

At first, procrastination prevented Ashley from calling Adam. Then toward the end of the second week, guilt set in. She'd waited too long to call.

He came. He didn't give up on me. He really is persistent. "I'm so glad to see you," greeted Ashley. "I've been meaning to call you, but I've been so busy." Adam had smiled forgivingly. Arrangements were made for the coming weekend. The complimentary ticket crutch wasn't needed. Adam's fear of rejection faded.

It took Ashley almost three months to work up enough courage to share her story about Brian. Until that time enjoying her time with Adam was haunted by guilt. *He seems so trustworthy. I really should open up to him.* She'd reasoned Adam had already figured out the most important things about her past life. He just missed the details. Adam hadn't brought up her past again. He really didn't need to know anything else. Her excuses weren't working.

Still, Ashley hated the idea of taking a chance, of trusting another man. She hated even more that she might again be proven incapable of accurately judging a man. Saying nothing meant she was safe. She wouldn't have made another mistake, at least a mistake that anyone else would know about.

One night, Ashley ended the ambivalence. "And that's why I cringe or jump sometimes. If I don't see your hand coming, I'm back in the living room feeling a fist in my face. I feel like I should run or scream or something."

"So this is okay?" Adam asked as he reached across the front seat of the car and held her hand in both of his. She nodded. He slid across the front seat closer to her. "And this?" His right hand softly touched the back of her head, gently stroking her hair while he brought his left hand closer to her far shoulder. Their lips met.

"I could see that coming too," she responded, smiling. They kissed again.

*   *   *

"It's your turn now," announced Stella as she cut into Ashley's past. Stella, with a hairbrush in hand, confirmed Ashley's earlier instructions on how her hair was to be done. By the time Ashley had cleared her head, she only caught the last part of the instructions but nodded in agreement, assuming the rest to be accurate. Glancing at her watch, she realized she'd still have at least an hour and a half to finish preparing for the dinner. *Plenty of time before Randy picks me up.*

When Ashley returned to her cabin, she set her evening clothes out on the bed and began putting on her makeup. *How perfect.* Her hair turned out just as she hoped. Her bangs curved out gracefully, coming to rest so that they just barely hid her eyebrows. The thick brown hair hung straight down but had a few of small waves for the discerning eye to catch. The tight curl at the tips of her hair rested just below her front shoulder blade. Depending on how she let her hair hang, most of the sides of her face could disappear, a suggestion of desired secrecy. She modeled the look. *Perfect for tonight.*

The reflection in the mirror showed a slender black dress with spaghetti straps. Ashley remembered the shopping trip that she, Danielle, and Carol had taken. The occasion was a twentieth wedding celebration for one of the office staff. The goal of this shopping adventure was to see which of the three could purchase the most attractive outfit. Depending upon how many times a certain new single loans officer looked their way or made a move on them would determine who was the winner. Ashley loved the way the dress clung to her body, accentuating a sexier figure than her two competitors'. It was a little shorter, but not much shorter than her rivals'. *It doesn't show as much cleavage as Danielle's dress. That's probably why she won.* Ashley and Carol each had to chip in 50 percent of the cost for Danielle's dress.

The three of them caught the eye of a number of married men too. They giggled and laughed all night. They had so much in common. Danielle was divorced from an unfaithful husband, and Carol had lost her husband in an automobile accident. The driver had a suspended license. They all lived alone and enjoyed being eyed by men but had little desire to get involved again. Danielle would only go out with a guy if he were buying. Carol, like Ashley, would go out with guys if they went out as a group. When Ashley began going out with Adam, Danielle was ecstatic after she heard it was his treat. "Hang on to that guy!" she exclaimed. Predictably, when Ashley e-mailed them about the great time she had in Barcelona, Danielle's response was, "Congratulations, you've landed yourself another rich one." Carol, however, was more interested in the kind of guy Randy was. They both asked to see a picture. *That's not going to happen,* thought Ashley. *I don't want any encouragement to get involved with Randy.*

Compared with Ashley's hairstyle, the dress revealed much more than she desired. She'd packed it the weekend that she booked the cruise. At their coffee break, they all talked about how much fun they might have if they dressed up like they had at the anniversary. Because it was at the bottom of her suitcase, she'd never thought of changing it for a more conservative outfit. "My shawl!" Ashley rummaged around in her souvenir bag. "Here it is. It's perfect." It was a white see-through material with black Spanish bulls all over it. Folding it as a scarf, tying around her neck, and letting it fall between her breasts produced a smile of satisfaction. Then Ashley draped it over her shoulders as a shawl, letting the balance hang. "Better yet." Using her fingernail clippers, she snipped off the price tag.

Ashley sat comfortably in her black dress, looking in the mirror at her matching silver earrings and necklace. *Ready, five minutes ahead of schedule. Perfect.*

Knock, knock, knock.

Ashley recognized it. *Randy already!* She checked the peephole and then opened the door.

"Wow! We don't need to go to dinner."

"Pardon me?" asked Ashley, a little surprised. *Why do you think I'm all dressed up?*

"Seeing you look so beautiful makes me feel like I've already received my reward for winning the match."

Ashley smiled and looked at Randy as he stood perfectly straight wearing his new light blue sweater with the navy Holland America logo on the left side. It coordinated well with his navy slacks and dark navy tie. Stretching from the top of the tie to almost the bottom in light blue was the Eiffel Tower.

"Think it's okay?"

"Perfect." Ashley turned around and went to the bed to slip on her comfortable low-heeled shoes. Then she grabbed her shawl and draped it around her shoulder as she had a couple of minutes ago. Turning around, she noted a disappointed look on Randy's face. "What's the matter?"

"You just hid that beautiful necklace! You sure you need your shawl?'

His response was so fast she almost believed him. "If I sit too close to the air-conditioning, I'll need it." Then seeing the sly grin on his face, she knew what he would rather see. Smiling at his obvious deviousness, she waved her hand toward the now-closed cabin door. "Let's go."

Randy arrived at a sectioned-off portion of the Pinnacle Grill with Ashley's hand on his arm. With his free hand, he showed the maître d' his invitation to the captain's table. Ashley's card was in her clutch purse along with her camera. The invitation card would be a souvenir. They were led to one side of the table, the side where the three table tennis winners sat. As the introductions went around, they discovered that the couples opposite them represented the first-, second-, or third-place winners in a digital photography contest. The winning photos, framed eight by ten, were on the wall behind the captain, who sat at the far end of the table. The first mate was to sit at the end next to Ashley, but he was to be a little late. Leaning close to Ashley, Randy whispered, "You were right. Everyone is dressed up." She smiled, accepting his recognition. "But you are the best-looking lady here." Under the table, she swatted his leg, and he smiled.

They each received their four-course menu. The selections were amazing. While they considered their choice, a waiter filled their glass with champagne. The half-emptied bottle of Nicolas

Feuillatte Épernay was placed on the table before Ashley and Randy. The waiter on the table tennis side took Ashley's order first: Master Chef Rudi's salad (selected baby greens surrounded with cucumber, bell pepper, and cherry tomatoes drizzled with a mustard cognac dressing); the appetizer was golden baked Brie in phyllo dough; the soup, lobster bisque and from the selection of seven entrées, Ashley pointed to the apricot-glazed salmon. The dessert choice was the easiest and the most popular—baked Alaska. Ashley asked the waiter if she could keep the menu to add to her souvenir collection.

"Of course." Randy echoed all her choices except for the appetizer and the entrée. His appetizer was the dialogue of salmon tartare with avocado (cold-smoked, pickled, and chipotle hot-smoked salmon with lime avocado tomato salsa), and the entrée was whole roasted tenderloin of beef.

After all the orders were taken, Captain Van Ryen rose. His official white captain's uniform contrasted with his relaxed smiling manner. "A toast. I salute some of my most talented guests aboard the *Eurodam*. I welcome you to the captain's table." He spoke with only a slight Dutch accent. After the clinking of glasses and a sip or two of the champagne, the captain made an applauded announcement. "On the menu, you may have seen two Holland America Commemorative wines: Chardonnay California 2005 and Cabernet Sauvignon California 2006. When you are served your appetizer, indicate to the waiter which bottle you prefer. That will be delivered to your cabin, compliments of Holland America Lines."

Wow, Mrs. Wassel never said anything about that, thought Ashley as she watched the captain enjoying the guests' responses. Speaking quietly in Randy's ear, she said, "You choose. You won. It doesn't matter to me."

Randy nodded. "And you choose the time and place where we'll share it."

The captain cleared his throat. "Perhaps while we are waiting for our food, we can learn a little something about each other. I would like to start with inviting each winner of the dinner invitation to share a little something about him or herself. In the case of the gentlemen to my right who took first prize in the photo contest, he can tell us something about his scene, why he chose it, or what his main passion or preoccupation is at home and where home is."

There was no hesitation. The midtwenties gentleman stood up and unbuttoned his dark suit jacket. *The captain must have already prepared him,* suspected Ashley. *He's too at ease.*

"My name is Robert, and I come from a small town in southern France." His heavy French accent drew more concentrated attention from Randy and Ashley. "Before I tell you about the picture I took and why I chose that setting, I would first like to propose a toast. To the captain and his crew, for making our holiday time aboard the *Eurodam* a truly enjoyable experience!" A chorus of affirmations joined the clinking glasses.

"Now as for my photo, what else would you expect of a Frenchman except to enjoy the appearance of attractive young ladies? So it was as I sat in the Crow's Nest. The bar scene you see here is only one of about fifty shots. My favorite one was when the lady's smile brightened her face as she sipped the signature drink of the day. I was able to catch the ceiling bar light reflecting off the shiny bar top. On the computer, I adjusted the light so her face and glass are highlighted. I managed to create a clear undistorted close-up. The dark black hair that framed her face and blended into the background was a bonus. I intended to submit that very picture until I looked at another shot about half a dozen frames later. It was a full-body shot of her sitting on the barstool with her legs crossed, sipping from her glass. Valentino, the bartender, could not be more pleased with the patron who adorned his bar. That photo became a serious contest contender too. When I put the two shots side by side to compare which I liked the best, I made a mistake of sliding the latter picture onto part of her black hair. I was surprised. By playing with the lighting, the second photo appeared as a reflection in her hair. I quickly saved it. I had my winner."

Ashley slipped her Pentax camera out of her purse just as the waiter placed her salad in front of her. Taking the hint, he offered to snap some pictures. "Whole table," she indicated so that the captain was included. "Then one of me from across the table." As her last request was fulfilled, she then pointed to Randy, signaling she wanted one of him too. He obliged. *When I get back, I can show the girls at work the guy I let get away.*

The second- and third-place photography winners each rose and told their stories. The appetizers came; and Randy, like others at the table, indicated his choice of wine. The ship's photographers entered, taking pictures of the table guests as well as the whole table. *Hoping to drum up a little more business*, predicted Ashley. *Well, I have my pictures already.*

A photographer was on the opposite side of the table when Randy stood up to do his introduction. He indicated he wanted his picture while he stood. When it was taken, he asked Ashley to stand up with him for a picture. At first, Ashley shook her head, but Randy insisted. Fearing her reluctance would create a scene, she stood up and smiled. She waved off a shot of her by herself. She had no intention of buying one.

"I live in Sherwood Park, a little city by the southeast corner of Edmonton, but I am the assistant manager at the north Edmonton Wholesale Warehouse on St. Albert Trail. It's a sporting goods distributor."

Ashley was startled. *That's about fifteen to twenty minutes from my place. When he said Sherwood Park, I thought I lived too far away from him for him to try and see me when we got back! My place wouldn't be that much farther for him than going to work.*

"My reason for being over in this part of the world is I am acting as a kind of manager for the soccer rep teams in the Greater

Edmonton area. The parents came together and chipped in for a special prize for the winning Edmonton rep team. They're paying for each of those players to be registered in the summer soccer training school in Barcelona this summer. It was my job to oversee their registration and to arrange for tours. The parents also contributed for my trip so I could plan an itinerary for the boys after their training. I'm pleased to say I finished my research just in time to take this wonderful cruise."

"I take it that soccer is big in Edmonton?" asked the captain.

"Not so much professionally, but much more so at the community level. Edmonton does draw some of the largest crowds in Canada for international soccer games." Randy could not help bragging a little about Edmonton.

The entrées came shortly after the next two introductions by the earlier table tennis winners. The table talk and, particularly, the answers the captain provided about the ship and some of the more unique experiences he encountered as a cruise captain made their time together pass quickly. The light creamy taste and the flaming presentation of the baked Alaska highlighted the dining time for Randy and Ashley, first-time cruisers.

"Often, after having feasted on a delicious meal such as we've just had tonight," began the captain, "I like to take a stroll on the promenade deck. It may be a bit breezy, but you'll see a beautiful evening sky." Like several of the other guests, Randy and Ashley headed for the deck doors.

Seeing the elevators, Randy said, "I've an idea. Let's go up to the Seaview Lounge. We'll have a better view of the night sky." As if the elevator thought it was a good idea, it opened its doors shortly after Randy pressed the button. "Now that's service," he said with a grin.

For a while, they stood by themselves near the railing, looking out into the night, determining where the distant black seawaters gave way to the star-dotted night sky. "In just three days, we'll have to give all this up," said Randy. He was standing so close to Ashley that he could feel the warmth of her body. Randy desperately wanted to put his arms around her and draw her in tight. He turned from the blank seascape, faced her, and hesitated, not daring to spoil the accepting mood.

"Yeeaah," sighed Ashley, turning to face him.

"Any plans when this is over?"

She shook her head. "You?" Wind whipped around, sending a few strands of hair across her face, tickling her cheek. A slight smile warmed her face. She enjoyed the sensation and the relaxed peaceful time they had together.

"Back home, soccer season will have already started." He looked up and stared at the moon as if gazing into a crystal ball. "I wouldn't be surprised to see Jasper Parks and his wife, Lynn, greeting me at the airport. They offered to give me a ride home—not because we're such great buddies, but because Jasper is the president of the Edmonton Boys Soccer Club. He'll be anxious to hear all about my trip. But he'll be even more interested when he can start booking me to talk to the soccer parents and then the boys. That'll mean dropping in at various practices and exhibition games. My appearances will be like dangling first prize in front of their eyes." He paused for a moment, still staring into space. "A great way to spur early game efforts."

"You look happy, eager to face what sounds like a demanding schedule."

"Seeing the smiles on the parents' faces, hearing the excited chatter bursting from the kids . . . It's wonderful. It's like having your own team win the finals." Randy glanced down at Ashley, catching sight of her sweeping back a small handful of hair that had become loose and hid her left eye. Vaguely, he recalled that action a couple of times while he had drifted into the future. "I know Jasper and Lynn had promised they'd give me about a week to get my feet under me when I get back before I'm invited to a dinner with the executive committee. Lynn will put on quite a spread. She usually does. Probably prime rib, if I know Jasper. That'll be my first briefing." Ashley swept the hair from her face again.

Randy interrupted his return anticipations. "Just a minute." He reached down and began to untie Ashley's shawl. She took a breath to object and started to slide away. He raised his index finger to stop her. She complied. Randy knew then he was right about not putting his arms around her earlier. He proceeded to undo the loose knot, slip her shawl off her shoulders, and fold it into a wide scarf.

A chill engulfed Ashley's shoulders. Was her discomfort from the slight temperature drop or the exposure of her low-cut evening dress? "Tilt your head back a little." A couple of his fingers swept back the stray hair that began hiding her face again. Then the converted scarf pinned down her playful hair. As if reading her thoughts, Randy slipped off his Holland America sweater and draped it around her bare shoulders, tying the arms and letting the sleeves drop, hiding her cleavage.

A smile slowly returned to brighten Ashley's face. *He's so thoughtful.*

"When you get back home, back to work, what are some of the highlights about the cruise that you will be sharing?" Randy intentionally shifted her attention.

I know Danielle and Carol are dying to hear all about you. "Ooh, I'll probably start by showing them the prints of my time in Barcelona. There's so much to tell about that day."

"It was great, wasn't it?"

"The bike tour, the lunch, the art museum. They were all terrific," Ashley fondly recalled without hesitation. "Thennn there was the carriage ride. It was the best."

I almost wrapped my arms around you. Randy confessed silently.

Ashley was careful to mention events, but not anything about Randy. That might open the door to an intimate conversation she did not want to explore.

"And then there is the sketch. You know, the day we played volleyball at the beach?"

"And the day I won the table tennis match and tonight's dinner."

"Yes, and tonight's dinner."

Ashley's top picks are all of times we spent together, Randy concluded. Her smile, her faster and more excited talk confirmed she loved those times. It was all the encouragement he needed to take a risk.

"I look forward to seeing the photos of the dinner. If they're any good, and I'm sure they will be, I plan to buy them, especially the one of you and me standing together at the dinner table." More people had joined them at the Seaview Lounge and near the rail.

"Oh, you're not."

"I am. I plan to frame the one of you and me."

"Don't be silly."

"I'm serious!" His tone confirmed it too. "Today has been one of the best days of the cruise."

Ashley had to tear her eyes from Randy's smiling face. She glanced at her watch. "If we're going to catch the late show, we'd better start heading in." Ashley sensed the intimate direction of this conversation and hoped to change the topic. She began walking toward the doors. Without hesitation, Randy followed her lead.

"So, any regrets about the cruise so far?" They had approached the elevators, and Ashley pressed the button.

"No, I don't think so." Ashley was taking Randy's sweater off and handing it to him.

"I have one," he said, accepting the sweater. Ashley didn't respond. With his free hand, he reached into his back pocket and pulled out a little blue coil-ringed notepad. "I haven't asked you for your phone number. I really would like to call you sometime when we get back." He flipped open the notepad and handed it to Ashley.

It's been such a wonderful evening. Why do you have to spoil it? When the pad was pushed even closer, Ashley accepted it. Randy's face lit up. *The face he had when he won the table tennis match*, recalled Ashley. His free hand plucked a pen from his shirt pocket. As he handed it to Ashley, a stretched-out "Pleeeaaaseee" underscored his request.

What do I do? How can I ruin his evening by refusing? Ashley looked at the dead elevator doors. They weren't coming to her rescue. They weren't offering an escape. The little table by the elevator doors holding a statue of a historic Roman citizen signaled plenty of room. Slowly, she placed the pad down on the table. *If he wanted to, he could always look up my phone number in the directory at home. There aren't that many Norrises in the book. I'm not unlisted. He's really asking permission to call me.* She clicked the pen to write. *I could put the wrong number down. Just one digit off so it would look like a mistake.* She began with the area code. It wasn't necessary. It was a stalling tactic. She wrote "458," the St. Albert area number. She looked up from the notepad.

He's thrilled. Her face flushed hot, turned red. *He's looking down the front of my dress? I don't have my shawl on.* She glanced down, embarrassed. She looked at the numbers already written down. *Should I rip the paper out of the book and throw it away?* After a moment's pause, Ashley looked at the pad, then scolded herself for her paranoia. *No, stupid, he's seen me in my bikini. Don't be so silly.* She double-checked the jubilant face again. *The overjoyed face of a winner, exactly what I saw when he won his chess match in the library two days ago. He thinks he's won, he's won me, like I'm some kind of a prize.* She looked up at him again, intending to show her disapproval of his narrow view of her that she'd conjured up.

Randy looked down, admiring Ashley. Patiently, he waited for her to work out her struggle. The image of a gentleman countered her excuse to not give her phone number. She smiled a thank-you for his understanding. *He's actually a very nice guy. Ooh, this is all too fast, too short a time. I can't decide now that I never want to see him again.*

And what would Adam say if I gave him my number? Adam's been so patient, so kind, so supporting. That's it! Adam is my way out! All I have to do is find a way of introducing Randy to my real boyfriend. Maybe I can bring Adam to do some shopping at the Wholesale Warehouse. I'll then introduce Adam to Randy as just a friend that I met on the cruise. I haven't really tried to be anything more than that to Randy. Ashley completed her phone number and returned the pad to Randy.

CPSIA information can be obtained at www.ICGtesting.com
Printed in the USA
LVOW052041160513

334186LV00001B/12/P